DADDY
hugs

igloobooks

You are the best Daddy ever because you take me on lots of adventures. When we walk through the sunny jungle, I hold on tightly to your tail.

You find the tastiest berries for me to eat and you
never tell me off when the sticky juice
goes all around my mouth.

Daddy, you are so much fun to play hide-and-seek with through the jungle trees, even though I know you always let me win.

Daddy, you are the best because when I tumble into a muddy puddle, you scoop me up and say, "There, there, never mind."

When it's time for a wash, you splash me with lovely,
cool water in the jungle lagoon and
spray me clean with your trunk.

When I am too little to climb up the next step on the rocky path, you are always there to help me and give me a big push.

You let me trumpet as loudly as I can
from the cliff top, even if some of the other
animals don't like it very much at all.

When it rains in giant splishes and sploshes, you let me hide underneath you so that I don't get too wet.

I love to sit with you and watch the purple and yellow sunset, especially when you tell me stories about all the animals that live in the jungle.

Daddy, I love you because when I am too
tired to walk, you swing me softly in
your long, curly trunk.

We have fun together all day long,
Daddy, but bedtime is the best.
You always hug me tightly as I fall
asleep under the starry sky.

Your soft, Daddy hugs make me feel so safe and warm. I am glad that you are my Daddy because you are the best.